German Shorthaired Pointers

Eric Reeder

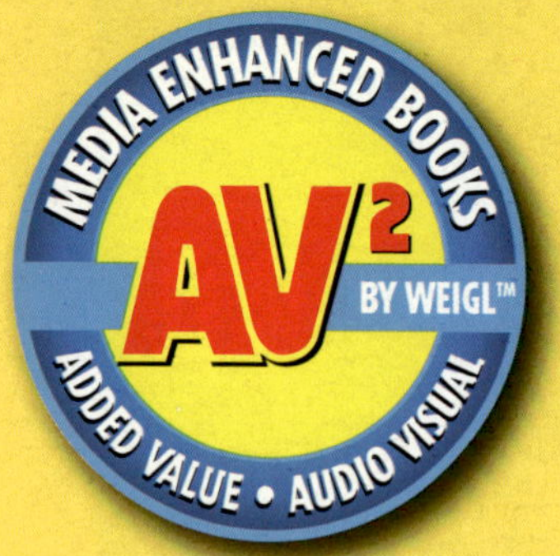

Go to **www.av2books.com**, and enter this book's unique code.

BOOK CODE

LBH75752

AV² by Weigl brings you media enhanced books that support active learning.

AV² provides enriched content that supplements and complements this book. Weigl's AV² books strive to create inspired learning and engage young minds in a total learning experience.

Your AV² Media Enhanced books come alive with...

Audio
Listen to sections of the book read aloud.

Key Words
Study vocabulary, and complete a matching word activity.

Video
Watch informative video clips.

Quizzes
Test your knowledge.

Embedded Weblinks
Gain additional information for research.

Slide Show
View images and captions, and prepare a presentation.

Try This!
Complete activities and hands-on experiments.

... and much, much more!

Published by AV² by Weigl
350 5th Avenue, 59th Floor
New York, NY 10118
Website: www.av2books.com

Library of Congress Control Number: 2017960034

ISBN 978-1-4896-7370-1 (hardcover)
ISBN 978-1-4896-7961-1 (softcover)
ISBN 978-1-4896-7371-8 (multi-user eBook)

Printed in the United States of America in Brainerd, Minnesota
1 2 3 4 5 6 7 8 9 0 22 21 20 19 18

012018
120817

Project Coordinator: John Willis Art Director: Terry Paulhus

Weigl acknowledges Getty Images and Alamy as its primary image suppliers for this title.

German Shorthaired Pointers

Contents

Name That Dog

What dog is the ideal hunting dog?

What dog needs a fence that is at least 6 feet (1.8 meters) tall?

What dog can do more types of work than most other dogs?

What dog might decide to chew up the carpet if it gets bored?

Did you say the German shorthaired pointer?

Then you are correct!

The Ideal Hunting Dog

Long ago, in the 1800s, hunters in Germany decided they wanted the best hunting dog possible. They mixed several different dog **breeds** together. These included the old Spanish pointer, the English pointer, the German tracking hound, and the English foxhound. All of these types of dogs have some traits that make them good hunters.

This new type of dog could hunt on land. It could also **retrieve** animals from the water. It was an excellent hunting dog.

Germany is a country in Europe. It is bordered by nine other countries.

This dog breed was brought to the United States in the early 1900s. Today, people who buy German shorthaired pointers like to know they are buying **purebred** dogs. Purebred dogs are often registered with organizations, such as the American Kennel Club (AKC). In 1930, the AKC added German shorthaired pointers as a new breed. By the 1940s, the German shorthaired pointer was a popular hunting dog in the United States. It is still a popular breed today.

German shorthaired pointers have been called the "every use dog." They were first called this in 1925 to promote the breed.

More than half of a German shorthaired pointer's weight comes from muscle.

Smart and Robust Dogs

German shorthaired pointers are smart dogs. They make great pets. Adult male German shorthaired pointers are about 23 to 25 inches (58 to 64 centimeters) tall at the shoulder. They weigh about 55 to 70 pounds (25 to 32 kilograms). Adult female German shorthaired pointers are usually smaller than males. Females are about 21 to 23 inches (53 to 58 cm) tall at the shoulder. They weigh about 45 to 60 pounds (20 to 27 kg).

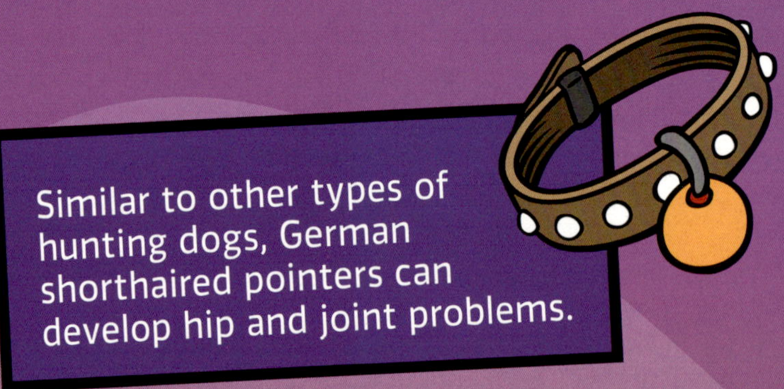

German shorthaired pointer fur is sometimes wiry or thick and can be a variety of colors. The most common color is a type of brown called "liver." This color can be anywhere from medium to dark brown. These dogs may also have spotted fur or fur that is solid black or white. Other possible fur colors are liver, black and white, black **roan**, liver and white, liver roan, and white and liver.

German shorthaired pointers have short, flat **coats** that keep water and dirt out. They have webbed paws. These act like paddles to help them move through the water. Their paws also have heavy, tough nails. These nails help German shorthaired pointers to grip and move in sand or dirt.

Black German shorthaired pointers are rare in the United States. They usually come from Germany.

What are Pointers Like?

German shorthaired pointers are active dogs with lots of energy. Sometimes, they may seem too excited or energetic. They are independent and have a mind of their own. Interesting sounds, smells, and sights can cause these dogs to lose focus. But they can be **trained** to behave. Owners of German shorthaired pointers have to know how to train and **discipline** them. Luckily, these dogs learn easily. They can also be trained to perform different tasks.

German shorthaired pointers are often trained to jump into water. Competitive dogs can jump distances up to 30 feet (9 m).

Pointers are great dogs for active owners or people who love to spend time outdoors.

If not trained, German shorthaired pointers can make a mess. They are smart enough to unlock kitchen cabinets to get into garbage cans.

These dogs make good pets. They are good with families and enjoy being around people. People who own German shorthaired pointers say they have great personalities. These dogs want to please their owners. They are also very **loyal**. However, they may bark at strangers and noises.

German shorthaired pointers like to jump and run. They are playful and fun. Some people train them to shake hands or do other tricks. German shorthaired pointers must be kept busy. If they are not, they will behave in ways that their owners will not like. If bored, they may chew up clothes or carpet. They might even destroy furniture.

Pointer Puppies

German shorthaired pointers often have many brothers and sisters. Sometimes, there are 12 or more puppies in one **litter**. During the first weeks of their lives, German shorthaired pointer puppies need to be **socialized**. If puppies are not socialized, they may be afraid of people and other animals.

In their first few weeks, puppies are cared for by their mothers. Their mothers feed and protect them. They keep their puppies safe. German shorthaired pointers should not be separated from their mothers before they are seven weeks old.

In 2017, the AKC ranked the German shorthaired pointer as the 11th most popular breed for families in the United States.

When German shorthaired pointers are puppies, they can start to be trained to play and fetch items. During this training, they need to be shown that their owner is in charge. Raising a German shorthaired pointer can be a lot of fun. It also takes a lot of time and effort from everyone in the family. Grown-ups and children can be involved with training a German shorthaired pointer.

A hunting dog's training can begin when it is eight weeks old.

Owners who want to train their pointers to help with hunting can begin with decoys or pretend animals.

Pointers Go to Work

German shorthaired pointers are smart dogs. They can do many different types of jobs. Most dogs cannot do as many different types of work as German shorthaired pointers can.

These dogs were bred to hunt. Hunting is still their main type of work. They can help hunt land and water **game**. German shorthaired pointers can hunt smaller game, such as rabbits and squirrels. They can also hunt larger game, such as deer. Sometimes, they retrieve game that their owners have hunted.

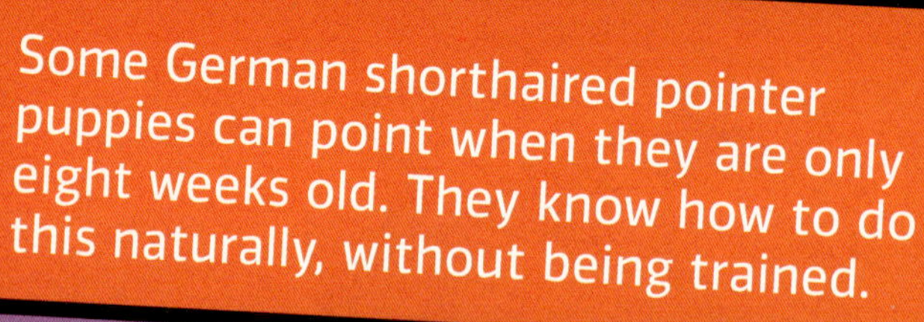

German shorthaired pointers use their bodies to point when they have found game. In the pointer pose, the dog is standing still. Its head is down, it is looking straight ahead, its front paw is lifted, and its tail is pointed upward. It holds its body in roughly the shape of an arrow. In this pose, it might point out a deer it has spotted for its owner. This is why these dogs are called pointers.

Other German shorthaired pointers are trained to be therapy dogs. They go to places such as hospitals and nursing homes. There, they help people in those places to feel calm. Some German shorthaired pointers are used as search-and-rescue dogs. They find people who are lost or trapped. They can also be trained to perform in dog shows.

It takes a disciplined dog to not chase an animal. German shorthaired pointers need months of training to perfect their pointing skills.

German shorthaired pointers are excellent swimmers. Most of them enjoy playing in the water.

Caring for a Pointer

Caring for German shorthaired pointers takes a lot of work. Like all dogs, they require food and water. German shorthaired pointers also need a great deal of exercise. Owners should make sure these dogs have lots of room to run and roam. A short daily walk is not enough for them. At least an hour of strong exercise every day is important.

German shorthaired pointers seem to always have energy. They enjoy running, hiking, jogging, and playing catch. Without exercise, they may become nervous. Lack of exercise can also cause problems with hips and other joints.

Bored German shorthaired pointers can escape. They need at least a 6-foot-tall (1.8 m) fence if they are going to be kept outside.

They can turn into badly behaved dogs if they do not have an owner who is determined and firm. They must be trained from the time they are puppies. They have to know that their owner is in charge. Luckily, German shorthaired pointers do well with training.

These dogs only need to be bathed once in a while. A bath once a month is often enough. Owners should also trim their nails as needed.

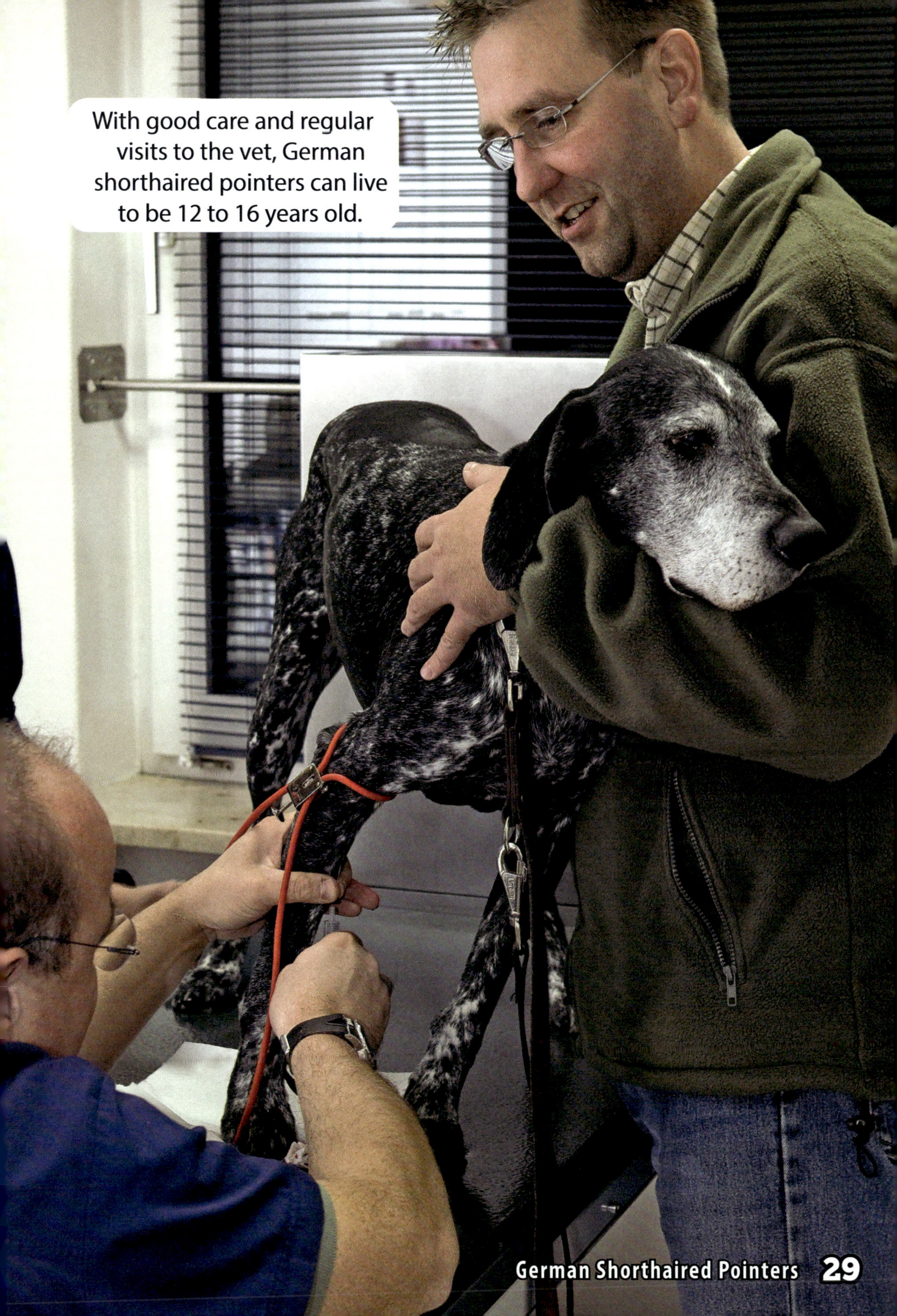

With good care and regular visits to the vet, German shorthaired pointers can live to be 12 to 16 years old.

Pointer Quiz

Q: How many puppies can be in litters of German shorthaired pointers?

A: 12

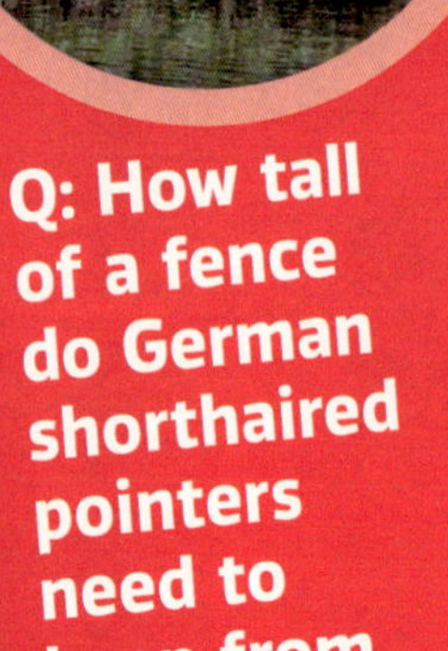

Q: How tall of a fence do German shorthaired pointers need to keep from getting out?

A: 6 feet (1.8 m)

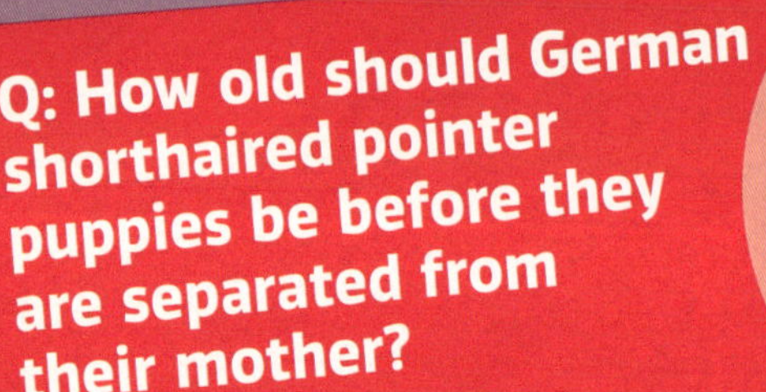

Q: How old should German shorthaired pointer puppies be before they are separated from their mother?

A: Seven weeks

Q: Why were German shorthaired pointers developed?

A: To be an ideal hunting dog

Q: What might German shorthaired pointers bark at?

A: Strangers and noises

Q: When did German shorthaired pointers become popular in the United States?

A: The 1940s

Key Words

breeds (BREEDS): specific types of dog

coats (KOTES): animals' fur

discipline (DIH-suh-plin): to train a dog to make it listen

game (GAYM): animals to be hunted

litter (LIH-tur): a group of baby animals born together

loyal (LOY-ul): devoted and faithful

purebred (PYOOR-bred): coming only from members of one breed

retrieve (rih-TREEV): to grab or fetch

roan (ROHN): having a coat with a main color that has a second color spread throughout

socialized (SOH-shul-izd): made used to and comfortable with other animals and people

trained (TRAYnd): to teach a skill or behavior

Index

Log on to www.av2books.com

AV² by Weigl brings you media enhanced books that support active learning. Go to www.av2books.com, and enter the special code found on page 2 of this book. You will gain access to enriched and enhanced content that supplements and complements this book. Content includes video, audio, weblinks, quizzes, a slide show, and activities.

AV² Online Navigation

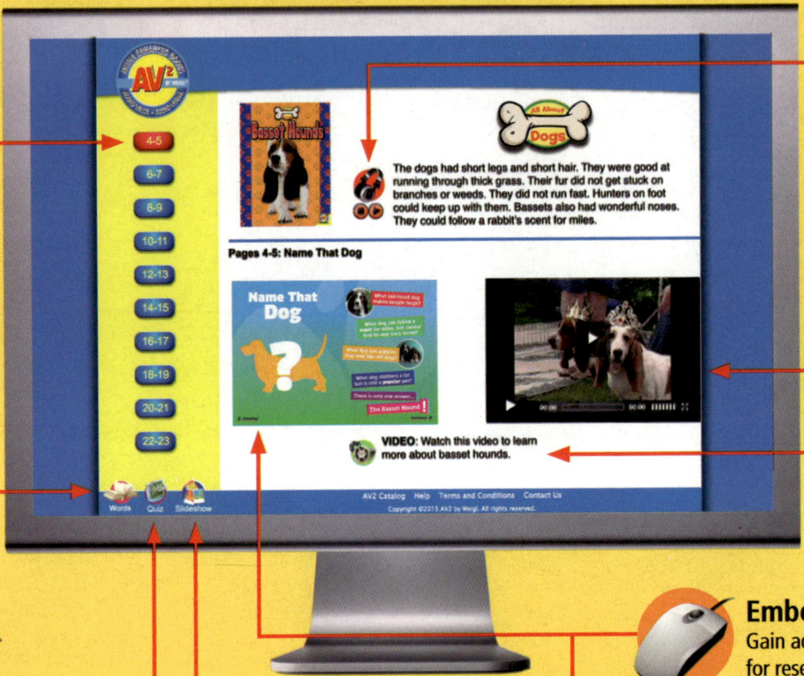

Audio
Listen to sections of the book read aloud.

Book Pages
AV² pages directly correspond to pages in the book.

Video
Watch informative video clips.

Embedded Weblinks
Gain additional information for research.

Key Words
Study vocabulary, and complete a matching word activity.

Try This!
Complete activities and hands-on experiments.

Quizzes
Test your knowledge.

Slide Show
View images and captions, and prepare a presentation.

AV² was built to bridge the gap between print and digital. We encourage you to tell us what you like and what you want to see in the future.

Sign up to be an AV² Ambassador at www.av2books.com/ambassador.

Due to the dynamic nature of the Internet, some of the URLs and activities provided as part of AV² by Weigl may have changed or ceased to exist. AV² by Weigl accepts no responsibility for any such changes. All media enhanced books are regularly monitored to update addresses and sites in a timely manner. Contact AV² by Weigl at 1-866-649-3445 or av2books@weigl.com with any questions, comments, or feedback.